# Enduring Love with Words and Art

Sunny Day

AuthorHouse™
1663 Liberty Drive
Bloomington, IN 47403
www.authorhouse.com
Phone: 1 (800) 839-8640

Published by AuthorHouse 03/18/2019

ISBN: 978-1-5462-7606-7 (sc)
ISBN: 978-1-5462-7607-4 (e)

Library of Congress Control Number: 2019900397

Print information available on the last page.

Any people depicted in stock imagery provided by Getty Images are models,
and such images are being used for illustrative purposes only.
Certain stock imagery © Getty Images.

This book is printed on acid-free paper.

authorHOUSE®

# Enduring Love with Words and Art

Lilly's goal: Resettling on Europa to help Earth's severe weather and ozone layer.

*A Viking's Dream*

I see a vision for my future life.
Row knots. Row faster.

The openness on water's roads,
Lead to different morning harbors.
Row knots. Row faster.

A gardener, in my own orchard,
I'll dance with smiling sunflowers
To nature's music.
Row knots. Row faster.

Life is holding me in awe.
Majestic sun on this moon comes.
Nautical miles, no more,
Newness, I'm here.
Row not. Live.

The desert and Europa soon harbor life using clay nanoparticles. Individuals living in the desert and on the satellite, Europa, try to help each other survive and enjoy living.

But first, Lilly must attend the newly established trade school for the arts.

The changing font styles and sizes with words and art express Lilly's and Coach Chuck's emotions and thoughts.

# Introduction

This third book in the *Learning and Growing* series begins with meeting Frank while driving to the mall.

Grandma's old boyfriend continually warned Lilly and Vicky to be careful when shopping in the mall. Frank didn't act like he was joking or kidding.

In any event, Lilly became frightened after Frank mentioned espionage and strangers in the mall.

No doubt, Frank would use espionage to stop Lilly and her friend's plans to repair the ozone and correct the Earth's severe weather.

Let's face the facts. Lilly was in the mood for romance and love and not espionage.

# Chapter 1

# New Ideas

"This is not funny, girls," Grandma Stormy said. "Please stop laughing."

Just then, someone approached their car and said, "I can help you, Stormy. Scoot over, and let me drive. The individual in front of you is protesting to the world about not having a place to park on this busy street."

As the man drove, Lilly smelled lemon, so she asked the newcomer, "Do you sell lemons or fish? And who are you?"

"My name is Frank. I dated your grandma until your grandpa, whose following us in my truck, won her."

"Let's not bore the girls with talking about the past. They want to do some shopping before they start high school tomorrow. These are my granddaughters, Lilly and Vicky."

"I am glad to meet you young ladies," Frank said while smiling. "When I'm not working for the government, I'm a chef at a new French restaurant named Le Poisson. We serve mostly fish like le salmon, le clam, also thin pancakes, la crepe."

"Are french fries originally from France?" Vicky asked.

"No. Back in the 1600s, potatoes were first fried in Belgium," Frank replied.

"Keep going in this direction, Frank. The mall is about twenty minutes from here. By the way, Karl and I are delighted you and your wife can stay with us for a few days. Do you still have your security clearance?"

"My federal security clearance is still active. You know, Stormy, there's always counterterrorism that deals with the military. I am always needed. My new boss is at the Department of Defense. I specialize in espionage."

Frank looked at the girls through the rearview mirror. "So be careful, young ladies. When you are shopping at the mall, do not talk with strangers. If anyone has seen you with me, you are now a person of interest for them to investigate by using government-owned GPS that's operated by the United States Air Force." Frank looked at the road and then back at the girls and said, "Just protect yourselves, girls, when you are out in public places."

"Oh, Frank, relax. You and Beverly never had children, so I can understand your safety concerns. If my grandbabies have any problems, they'll telephone. They know how to use your GPS system," Stormy said.

"Still, remember, young ladies, eyes are everywhere," Frank warned.

"Relax, Frank," Stormy said. "The girls know about safety rules and our family values. Let's not go overboard to inform them about things that may never happen. They will be safe alone in the mall."

One sleepy but now scared passenger yawned and nodded her head. Was Le Poisson's real purpose to deal with fish flavored with lemon juice or for espionage that used heat to reveal the lemon juice writing?

If only Lilly could exercise to calm herself. She was still trying to cope with her father's death and adjust to her mother quickly marrying another Navy SEAL.

Worrying about her height also tarnished her self-esteem. She worried new friends and teachers would laugh at her height.

Adding to her worries, Lilly began to fret about never finding a career.

What was her purpose in life?

Suddenly, the white noise in the moving car began to magnify Lilly's new fear: espionage. Something dangerous just might happen in the mall.

If only Lilly could be in a safe place. In Australia, young kolas were always safe on their mothers' backs.

But she wasn't a kola or a mommy's girl. She wished her father was still alive and with her. He'd explain dating and her height in a positive way. He'd also understand the connection her height had with a career that would fulfill her purpose in life.

But before Lilly knew it, she was not with her father or in Australia. She and her sister were at the mall.

# Chapter 2

# Espionage in White Noise

The two girls happily walked inside the shopping mall. Each one had been given her allowance and a few additional dollars. Labor Day sales were everywhere.

While they were window-shopping for shoes, Lilly felt a sharp sting on the right side of her neck.

Before she was able to check out the now burning sensation, a group of people brushed against the outside of her left arm while making distracting *whisk*, *whisk*, *whisk* sounds.

Vicky, already inside the shoe store, was motioning for Lilly to hurry and join her.

So Lilly quickly went into the shoe store and forgot about the sting.

Hours later, their dad, David, picked up the sisters with their packages.

Once home, he said he'd walk Lilly's dog.

Entering the dining room, Vicky noted her grandpa was already seated at the table. "Why are you early, Grandpa?" she asked.

With an ear-to-ear grin, he replied, "I am early because this is a special day—a day never to be forgotten. This day calls for a celebration. It's my birthday. I'm anxious for the celebration to begin."

Suddenly, his grin turned into a serious look. His hawk vision had spotted the tiny red dot on Lilly's neck.

Quickly, he pushed himself away from the dining room table. Standing up, he gently touched her neck. "What happened? Where were you? What did it feel like when it occurred? How many people touched you after you felt the sting?" he questioned in a machine-gun, quick-firing format.

Sunny, Lilly and Vicky's mother, walked into the room and screamed, "Oh no! Not my poor baby. She's marked for life!"

Everyone's eyes were now on Lilly's neck and the red spot as David entered the room. He said, "Lilly, soon your mono will have run its course. You'll be in shape to walk your dog."

Seeing tear-stained faces and then Lilly's red spot, the dad's mood quickly changed. Slowly, he carefully touched his daughter's neck—and her future.

"Am I going to die? Why is everyone so anxious and upset? Are the spies who are feared everywhere now after me? Am I now a tool for espionage?" Lilly asked.

"Exactly, Lilly. You are a marked tool for espionage, or 18 US Code Chapter 37," David said. "The issue of concern for you, Lilly, is not freedom of speech. It is freedom of thought."

Lilly was stunned twice—once in the mall and now with her dad's words.

Lilly's dog, Bella, stood at her left in a guard stance. Also sensing danger, Cuddles, Vicky's cat, ran from the room to hide in a closet.

Just then, Aunt Charlotte and her nephew, Ed, entered the dining room. Upon seeing the red spot on Lilly's neck, the aunt gasped, "Espionage!"

"Why was Lilly targeted?" Ed asked. "Will I be next?"

"I do not have the answers, Ed," Aunt Charlotte replied. "Somehow, someone has discovered Lilly's ability to see pictures of people's thoughts. Just by rubbing elbows with Lilly, certain individuals will know exactly what she and others she has talked with are thinking."

Grandpa Karl added, "I bet everyone any amount of money that group wants to duplicate Lilly's neurons."

"I wonder if they also want to discover the way Lilly and Vicky code messages to each other," the girls' dad said. "The Navajo code talkers designed a similar unbreakable code. Even the Marine Corps staff was unable to understand the code. Finally, in 2007, a Congressional bill was passed. It recognized all American Indians who were code talkers during the two world wars."

Aunt Charlotte commented, "Lilly and Vicky have used their knowledge of languages to invent another type of unbreakable code. Possibly, the girls will have careers as language interpreters."

"That's an idea," Vicky said.

"In any event"—David shuddered—"Lilly has been given a red spot from a microchip that's the size of a grain of rice. Now Lilly's exact location will always be known, as well as her every thought."

Suddenly, Ed said, "This reminds me of Robert Louis Stevenson's paper with a black spot on one side and a message written on the other side. Lilly should not act frightened like Billy Bones."

Looking directly at his cousin, Ed added, "Lilly, you need to remain calm like Long John Silver. Your buried treasure is not gold hidden on an island but knowledge in your head. Your knowledge and ability to see people's thoughts as photographs might make for a useful government career."

"Let's not worry," Grandpa Karl said. "Now hold still so I can remove the stinger with tweezers."

"Oh, for goodness sakes. Those bees are still after me," Lilly giggled. "I trained bees to recognize my face. They must need some sweet attention."

Just then, the car's movements had stopped, and so did her dream.

It had been decided not to go to the mall but to go home. Lilly was still recuperating from mono. Frank's warning of danger and mentioning espionage had caused Lilly's dream.

When Lilly opened her eyes, she saw Frank again, smiling.

"Lighten up, Lilly. Don't let your imagination and fears control your life," Frank said. "While you dozed, your restless legs syndrome kept everyone guessing just where you were trying to go."

To change the topic and get her mind away from dangers, Lilly asked, "Just what do you do for a living, sir?"

"I'm no chef, Lilly. That lemon fragrance was from drinking a glass of lemonade. I fear to imagine just what you might have dreamed if I told you about other military inventions."

"Besides GPS, what other things did you and the military invent?" Grandma Stormy asked.

"Well, Jeeps, EpiPens, freeze-drying techniques, microwaves, flying cars, artificial gravity, hover bikes, hover trains, lasers, Tasers, and space communication. I also need to mention low-light photography, since you girls are interested in taking pictures at night."

"Anything else, sir?" Vicky asked.

"Now, let me think. Yup. There's nuclear medicine, wireless long-range electronic shock tools, cameras, and nuclear photonic rockets. I heard you girls are interested in Europa and Titan. Check out current military inventions used for space exploration."

Lilly was exhausted, so she only replied, "Thanks. For certain, we will use duct tape."

Vicky chimed in. "We'll also use aviator sunglasses that were invented for pilots."

"Like the military, we plan to use superglue for wounds," Lilly added. Then she was quiet. She didn't have enough energy to ask again what Frank did for a living and why he was visiting her grandparents, possibly to celebrate her grandpa's birthday.

As Lilly entered her home, she began thinking about her new school.

In the past, the LOVE group of friends, Lilly, Oliver, Vicky, and Ed attended the same school.

This year, only Oliver and Ed would be together in a high school that stressed science and math. Vicky would attend a high school for languages.

Lilly would be in a high school that was her second choice. Without her friends and therapy dog, she had no one to comfort her when her imagination and intelligence got the best of her.

Boy, she wished she was old enough to join the US Navy. Whatever the challenge or mission might be, Lilly would have navy buddies nearby.

Possibly, sketching water and boats or writing poems might distract her. Lilly wished for the good old days that she had shared with her father and friends. Equally important, Lilly wished to fall in love.

# Chapter 3

# High School, Another Hormone City

Early the next morning, Lilly was saying, "Mi llama Lilly," in her Spanish class. Lilly felt that class was practical and enjoyable.

Her next class, English, was located a distance from the Spanish classroom. The experienced writer didn't want to be late for her gifted English class.

Already, she was able to write a solid argument and read critically, and she knew literature. What would be challenging was producing writings for publication.

Gliding with grace and tall beauty, Lilly was seen by the basketball coach who was also the track coach.

Lilly was also seen by Aaron, an elementary friend. When Aaron's family relocated, PCS (permanent change of station) in military terms, to a different state, the friends lost contact with each other.

In the past, Aaron had helped Lilly learn to relax after her father was killed. The military's wraparound services and other support services also helped Lilly cope with her loss.

But when another Navy SEAL planned to enter Lilly's life as a new dad, Lilly felt she would lose her mother and all memories of her father. And to intensify the loss, Lilly wasn't able to understand her mother suddenly forgetting her father and wanting to marry another Navy SEAL.

But that morning, Lilly wasn't thinking about her father or her mother. Her mind was occupied with not being late for class.

There in a high school hall, Lilly found it easy to quickly walk to class and say yes for track and no for basketball.

The coach had asked Lilly to use her superior height on the basketball and track teams. The coach was even willing to rebuild Lilly's muscles, which were still recuperating from mono. Lilly felt the coach clearly understood her goals. For sports, her height was a gift.

Still, while she was hurrying to class, Lilly again thought new friends and new teachers wouldn't accept her. Besides, what male would be attracted to the tallest female freshman in their high school?

At the exact moment Lilly was dealing with her fear of no male wanting to date a tall female, Cupid saw Lilly and Aaron walking together to their class. Lilly was three inches above the very tall, lanky Aaron. Both were rushing in an unknown world that had Cupid smiling.

That early morning, Cupid was looking for young hearts to make love connections. If unsuspecting teens weren't seeking love, he'd use his full note to draw them into his love arrows.

Cupid is always observant. He knows what he is doing with youths, especially youths who didn't realize the consequences of their actions. Let's face it. For every action, there's a reaction.

In that high school, like in many other high schools that Cupid visited, Cupid did not require archery skills. Many young hearts, not paying attention to their actions, simply walked into his arrows, which had powers to not only create love but hate.

Lilly's love and compassion were more powerful than hate, so Cupid would need to use jealousy. And what stories jealousy has told.

In Greek mythology, there is a story about the goddess of weaving, Athena, who challenged Arachne to a weaving contest. Arachne won. Jealousy had Athena ruining Arachne's weaving. Feeling pity for herself, Arachne hung herself. Athena then felt remorse and turned Arachne into a spider. Even today, spiders are recognized for their weaving. Note that spiders aren't seeking attention through their weaving.

But was Lilly seeking attention in high school? She was lovely, graceful, and breathtaking and didn't dress like the average female in school. Lilly enjoyed wearing a long, flowing skirt with a blouse, which she then partially covered with an apron. Her feet enjoyed sneakers with the fronts removed so her toes could breathe and wiggle. The shoelaces were replaced with colored ribbons that matched the color of her blouse.

When Aaron had first seen Lilly, he was shocked and powerless. He hadn't seen her since sixth grade. At that time, Lilly was the shortest one on all of the swim teams.

"Once we were on the same swim team," he was finally able to utter. "My twin sister, Lisa, and I helped you with your loss and confidence."

"Thanks again for that, Aaron. I'm almost late for my next class. Let's talk later," Lilly said.

Oblivious to everything but time, Lilly entered her English classroom. She had been followed by Aaron and other lovesick puppies. Upon entering the room, some immediately backtracked to different classrooms.

Everyone but Aaron was seated. He simply stood like a Trojan horse by Lilly's chair. Aaron was planning a battle of words to capture Lilly's heart and math mind.

Sensing an unseen problem about to happen, the new teacher announced, "Anyone not seated before the bell rings will be counted late."

Everything that Lilly heard for most of the class time bored her until she heard William Shakespeare. The British poet, actor, and playwright was regarded as the world's greatest writer in the English language. Lilly was not from his world.

Not able to contain herself for another minute, Lilly blurted, "*Hamlet*, *Macbeth*, and *Romeo and Juliet* may have been some of his best plays in his day. Certainly, he shouldn't be considered for this twenty-first century, the third millennium. We don't need to be taught disobedience and betrayal. In a weekend, there's love, out of love, marriage, and murder. To top things, William Shakespeare advocated using suicide to solve problems."

Looking directly at her teacher, she continued explaining her views. "Great writers not only use words, but they use their ideas that are set with morals and values."

Before Miss Taylor could come out of the corner with a reply, Lilly was saved by the bell. The new teacher would need a plan, with faculty advice, to be ready for another encounter from the magnet beauty with independent reasoning.

Lilly's next class was math.

For some, it was general knowledge. For Lilly, it was just a noun. If only Lilly might discover a use for math. She disliked showing her work unless it was necessary for her plans to settle people on Europa.

Later, she relaxed using daydreams in art and then health class. Soon, it was time for lunch.

Lilly had been enjoying her sandwich until Aaron approached her with two of his buddies.

Earlier, Aaron had informed his pals of his powers over Lilly.

"Watch this expert knock Lilly of her chair. I had coached her in grade school to quiet her nerves and get centered for several swim meets," Aaron boasted. "I even know how to excite that helpless beauty."

"Why not win her over this time in a civilized fashion?" one buddy asked.

"Lilly was the best in our sixth-grade math class. I need to know how she knew the answers without showing her work," Aaron replied. "Somehow, Lilly used shortcuts that provided correct answers. Even in this high school's remedial math class, Lilly doesn't show her work but has correct answers. I want in on whatever enabled her to score hundreds, 100 percent of the time."

After winking one eye at Lilly, he began instructing his buddies. "Now, men, just listen to this top gun sing. Use the words I have written for you on these papers. Follow my lead, men."

"For Lilly's pleasure," one said, "we will sing to the fair lady."

Smiling, Lilly continued to slowly eat while two members of the trio began reading words Aaron knew by heart.

The trio clicked their fingers to provide intensity for the six-syllable lines:

The best of the morning,
was seeing your beauty.
With weak knees, we stumbled.

We're not traffic cops, but
it's citizen's arrest
For the illegal act
of wrecking our young hearts.

It's an open and shut case,
no attorney can help.
Nor doctor's surgery.

Take our legal advice,
And date your friend Aaron.

Softly she replied, "Don't exaggerate. I only saw three brave knights on bended knees bowing to royalty, Lilly."

Aaron quickly responded. "Embrace change in your life. Dream not. Be alive. This is no school or house for the dead. Live not with fear, fair lady. You need to take a new step. Like in the movie, be a tightrope walker. Take a chance to live and to love."

Lilly replied with a soft voice. "It's the twenty-first century. Wake up; stop daydreaming of conquests. Use Google to connect with today's life, Sir Aaron and friends. I'm like a free, wild panda with a dangerous bite. I also have my DNA. My Scandinavian father had Viking ancestors, true warriors. I am an independent Viking and aquatic mermaid, not a fish out of water for one of your planned future folklores. Cast your lines elsewhere."

With her napkin, Lilly dabbed her lips and then said nothing. She had finished eating.

This was a school for the arts, including music for her eating pleasures.

Lilly chose not to say more or supply a ticket for others' entertainment. She closed all doors for more words by simply walking away.

At the correct time, if need be, Lilly would respond with the appropriate words. Lilly was determined not to be like John Keats's bride of quietness, frozen in time. She was alive, not a figure on a Grecian urn.

Besides, Lilly needed her energy to plan a ranch for Native American Indians and active military members to use during the summer. At the ranch, there would be activities. Possibly a play about teen love—anything but another William Shakespeare tragedy.

She really wished Aaron would help at the ranch. They might just be friends like they were in grade school—just friends.

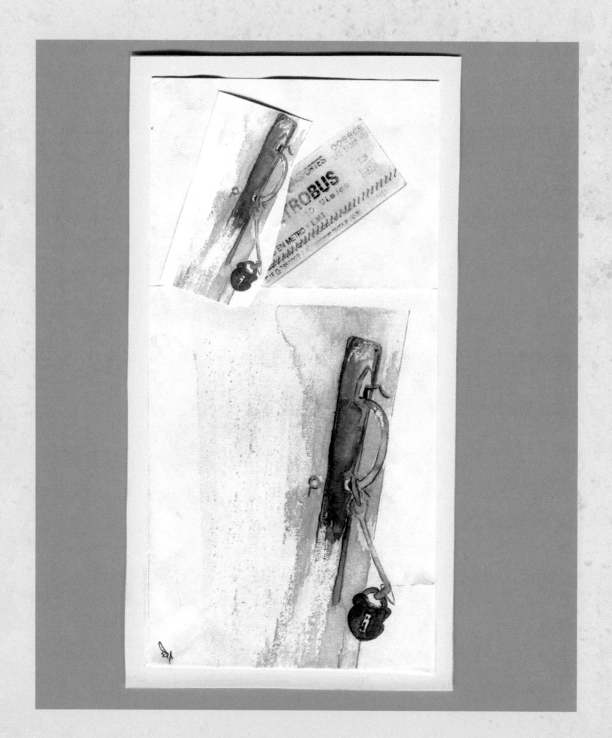

# Chapter 4

# Dream or Not Dream

Entering science class, Lilly saw a youthful, redheaded teacher named Miss French.

The teacher shared what she knew about them and their favorite style of learning. "I will be observing ways that you gather information using your senses or your intuition. With the information, you might make decisions using thinking or feeling. This class uses thinking."

Smiling, she then added, "To balance personalities and not disregard the needs of others, or my teaching time, I am using a minute for each student to answer a question or to read his or her written answer. My laptop will help me keep time records."

Pointing to the smart board screen, she read, "In 2016, Bloomberg rated Russia's higher education as being the third best in the world. If a student didn't take notes while in class, they'd be asked to leave the class. I won't do that."

Pointing to several students' notebooks, she added, "Instead, you will be given an open notebook quiz that has questions you can answer using your class notes. If you happened to be absent before an unannounced quiz day, I'll provide notes for you to use. By the way, I'd advise you to take notes not only when I'm lecturing, but when you are viewing films or smart board presentations and even other students' answers."

Moving to her desk, she began the lesson.

"Dmitri Mendeleev was a Russian chemist and inventor. He had designed the periodic law. He used the law to correct the properties of some of the fifty-six already known elements of his time. He also used the law to predict the properties of yet-to-be-discovered elements. In 1869, Dmitri Mendeleev arranged the chemical elements into groups after his *dream* that helped him realize the physical and the chemical properties were related to their atomic mass with similar properties."

Pointing to the chart on the back wall, she continued. "Today, the table has 118 confirmed elements. The chemical groups are listed vertically. I might even discuss elements not listed, like unbinilium. It is also known as eka-radium or simply element 120. This school is for challenging you to solve Earth's problems. Science, math, and clouds, in my opinion, are needed. However, the principal is predicting your creativity and dreams will find the answers."

Nodding her head, she continued speaking. "Still, as a scientist, I am fascinated how the sleeping mind can solve problems. In 1818, Mary Godwin (Shelley) had a dream to get ideas for writing with her girlfriends. Her dream was about the creation of a new male. That dream produced the first written science fiction novel titled *Frankenstein*."

Several students gave each other monster gestures and only spoke to each other with bulging eyes and changing body postures.

"Alfred Russel Wallace's tropical fever caused an extreme dream and helped him understand natural selection. And Otto Loewi, the father of neuroscience, used dreams to understand that the signaling across synapses was a chemical event. In 1936, a Nobel Prize in medicine was given to him for his dream."

Walking over to Lilly's table, she continued speaking. "I'll probably never use dreams to solve problems, but that doesn't mean you couldn't use your imagination and dreams to solve our depleting ozone and climate change problems. I believe the solution has a lot to do with Earth's clouds."

Picking up her textbook, students were instructed to first read the chapter about clouds. Then they were to write a poem to introduce themselves and the cloud they imagined being.

"You may also describe another cloud in your poem for extra credit. The main task is for you to know something about one cloud and then learn about other clouds from other students. Your poem helps me recall your name using a technique called association."

Lilly chose to write a poem to describe her rapid growth in height, her values, and her imagination.

The second cloud's description was to deflate Aaron's confidence and sixth-grade control over her by using the word *reign* versus the word *rain*. Lilly's last line not only suggested her height but her standards.

Several students, having completed the assignment, began daydreaming, while others used their journals to doodle drawings. Doodling helps one not think too much or think too little. It can help one focus.

Lilly chose not to daydream. She'd use her extra time to finish sketching kola bears in her art journal. Besides, she wasn't interested in seventeenth-century doodling.

After fifteen minutes, Lilly was asked to begin the introductions. She introduced herself as *Just Cumulus*, using eight-syllable lines in her poem titled "Lilly Doesn't Date Pollution."

Lilly Doesn't Date Pollution.

Pay attention to what you see.
Starting low, then growing up high,
Imagination can play tricks.
Animal shape or people clouds
Are not real, just cumulus.

Pay attention to who you are.
Your mineral core and light reign
Lives and moves in cold atmospheres,
Flat, hazy, featureless stratus.

Pay attention to who I am.
Go back to your artic region.
Play with energy emissions.
Don't need you, a wild card for change.

Pay attention to who I am.
Starting low, then growing up high,

Even time-lapse photography
Shows relationship fact of life.
Lilly's an unreachable cloud.


    Other students then read their poems.

    When it was Aaron's turn, he described himself as Sir Cirrus with curling locks of hair just like Aaron's hair.

    Lilly blurted out, "Love and those clouds don't last long." That made Lilly laugh and the class giggle.

# Chapter 5

# Geography for Answers

All day, Lilly had been waiting for geography to give her ideas for sending messages into space with Oliver, Vicky, and Ed.

For more than fifty years, people have been looking for extraterrestrial life using radio messages. Since grade school, Lilly and her friends had been attempting to do the same thing.

The first message from adults on Earth had been sent in 1974. That message used two prime numbers. If the viewer saw the message as a 23-by-73 grid, then a series of simple pictures might be seen. The message was sent using an Arecibo radio telescope.

In about 1999, messages, again, had been sent into space using the Ukraine RT-70 radio astronomical telescope.

The group wouldn't duplicate those early messages or later messages sent on *Voyager*'s two golden phonograph records.

But first, Lilly, Oliver, Vicky, and Ed needed an energy efficient way of sending their message to the cosmos to help Earth's depleting ozone and extreme weather conditions. In a few weeks, the group of friends planned to meet to share their individual theories.

Mr. Hill took attendance and then began his lecture.

"The third largest continent is North America. It has one-third of Earth's population. The forty-nine United States are in four geographical regions: the Northeast, the South, the Midwest, and the Northwest. Hawaii, the fiftieth state, is located in the Pacific area."

Pointing to the smart board's picture, he continued explaining. "Earth's *interior* is *younger* than the planet. About 4.5 billion years ago, the uniform ball of hot rock underwent changes: compression, accretion, and collision. The changes caused temperatures inside the ball to increase. It took 500 million years for the increased temperatures to melt the iron to produce silicates, water, and air."

Mr. Hill explained the melted iron, nickel, and other heavy metals had moved to the center of the ball. Because Earth rotates with a liquid swirling metal interior, an electrical field is produced that helps life on the planet survive. Lilly believed that electrical field was the energy source needed to send their messages.

Suddenly, Mr. Hill stopped talking. He had intercepted a note that was created for Lilly.

Motionless, Lilly heard her teacher read Aaron's ten-syllable lines, his head titled.

My Young Heart Will Always Be Yours, Lilly.

Waves against seconds in liquid spaces,

An engine against time, my heart sped up
In the competitor's crawl swim event.

Never needing air, ahead you did swim
In competition's front crawl and my heart.
As you resisted breathing, surfacing,
Your two hands rose, touched competitor's wall.
At our team's winning gold medal event,
Love, my young heart's fate suddenly was yours.

Everyone in the class laughed—everyone but embarrassed Lilly. This time, Aaron had the last laugh with the class giggling in close pursuit.

"That's enough, everyone," the teacher said. "This geography class and other classes are hoping you will be able to solve Earth's ozone problem and severe weather conditions. Some teachers think it's all due to Earth's shifting magnetic field. In my opinion, the Earth's *magnetic* field *flips* isn't the cause. I won't talk any more about it unless you have ideas for a new magnet compass."

Walking over to his work table, he continued talking. "Now, please look at this displacement map while I explain how mountains are formed."

When the class ended, Lilly left the room. The sound of giggles from other students laughing at her hurt her pride.

# Chapter 6

# Adult Help

After school, Lilly was relieved to see her grandma. Her mother had a part-time job and wouldn't be home for several hours. Lilly and her stepsister would be cared for by their grandma. Their dad was still TDI for special training.

Even before school had begun, Vicky and Lilly had discussed the Earth's resonances and 7.83Hz frequency to repair the ozone and severe weather conditions.

Vicky had suggested using electrical currents from lightning. The electricity would produce new-air music to *rebuild* the ozone using lightning that is made in the *inter-* and *intra-*clouds.

Thinking about William Thomson (Kelvin) and Rudolf Clausius's second law of thermodynamics, Lilly had asked her sister, "Wouldn't energy be lost along the way? Time does change music and the weather."

"If everything decays, and there would be disorder, how can you help solve the problems?" Vicky asked. "Using your birds' voices?"

"Earth's orbiting around the sun with a tilted axis, causes some of Earth's circular surfaces to receive more heat—radiation," Lilly replied. "I plan to use Europa and other asteroids to balance the temperatures."

While shaking her head, Lilly added, "Your repairing the ozone hole may worsen global warming. That ozone hole causes the formation of brighter-than-usual clouds. Those clouds shield the Antarctic region from greenhouse gas emission. High-speed winds sweep up sea salt to form moist clouds. Those clouds reflect the sunrays that would otherwise warm the Antarctic air. I'm suggesting asteroids to block sunlight for regional coverage."

Vicky agreed. She then thought about another use for the clouds in the troposphere. Her rain clouds might be moved to deserts. The lightning would also separate the nitrogen atoms in the air to form nitrates, a type of fertilizer.

It would be up to Lilly to figure out a way for desert plants to use that nitrate fertilizer. Both sisters agreed about using deserts as places for people to live and produce their food. Basically, Earth has 71 percent oceans, and the remaining 29 percent is land—33 percent of that land is desert.

That afternoon, Lilly was relieved that her sister was at band practice. Lilly needed time alone with their grandma to explain her problem.

"So," Grandma said, "you aren't looking for a keeper of fire but a distinguisher of flames. First, I will telephone your school and speak with two of your teachers and explain your need for their help. Because opposites attract, the petite, nondreamer science teacher, Miss French, and the muscular, dreamer coach, Chuck, will be a motivated team to help you. A teacher's job is not only to teach but to protect students."

Hugging her granddaughter, Stormy explained her plan. "I'll let your parents know about the meeting. Second, I'll ask your parents if we can find a new physician for you. Your health needs to be reevaluated. You are stressed out and appear to have less energy to meet the challenges that are a part of daily living. The new physician will let us know when you can begin exercising. Exercise will increase your appetite."

"I am hungry. I'm not eating a lot because I want to stop growing. Did you know that I'm even taller than many of my teachers?" Lilly asked.

"A new physician needs to be consulted. Your parents are supplementing your diet with vitamins and pep talks. Still, natural foods are not only safe but help bones store calcium. You need to be aware of bone density. Please, Lilly, don't carelessly ruin your body worrying about God's plans for your height."

"I have another problem. I don't like the school that I'm attending," Lilly said.

"Not showing your math work prevented you from attending your first choice of schools—a math and science charter high school," Grandma said. "Testers can't understand you. Are you guessing or intuitively calculating? But I know what you're doing. You've been using the slide ruler I gave you in sixth grade. Over the past two years, you have mastered the art of visually calculating with your mind's slide ruler."

Lilly giggled in response.

"Now, would you like to hear what is really wrong with your school? Can you handle some honest comments?" Grandma asked.

"Oh, for goodness sakes, you should know me by now. I seldom disagree with you for long. My right eye is following your every word."

"Another thing that has you not liking your school is Lisa JP. She is in the same science and math classes as Oliver and Ed. Also, she's their lab partner. No doubt, you are jealous she's their new friend."

"Wow, Grandma, you're good!"

"I'm sensing that at one future point in time, the group will discuss things with you for your intuitive input. You'll need math to not only prove your ideas but to help others understand and see your ideas. That will be the time you knock their socks off with math."

"Two, three, or four socks? Just how many socks will I be able to knock off?" Lilly asked.

"Let's wait until later to discuss those numbers. Tomorrow, I'll also speak with your math teacher and drop ideas about motivating you with binary numbers. Now, what about having a snack and taking a break with a story? *The Three Bears* might be an enjoyable book for us to reread together and change words just for fun."

"Did you know, Grandma, that in 1837 Robert Southey inspired cartoons, poetry, and even movies with that bears story? Anyway, in his story, the bears moved to the girl's home, which was her grandmother's home, to learn how to dust and clean. Those were domestic values a young lady was expected to master during that culture's time."

"Lilly, the very first book had been written by Eleanor Muir in 1831 for her nephew's fourth birthday," Grandma said. "During that period in American history, witches were feared. We can presume the old lady, in the original story, was a witch because she was caught and then burned. The old lady lived, so she was impaled on a church steeple. That was some story for a four-year-old's birthday gift."

"I understand changing times needed different happenings and characters," Lilly noted. "Even Walt Disney changed stories. Fairy tales were sources for his films."

"When you were learning to read, I read you *The Gingerbread Man* to have you practice sequencing events. You also enjoyed *The Ugly Duckling*. Possibly, that is a tale you need to think about since your inside beauty is stretching you." Then she noted, "Life is also about knowing how to talk."

"But I'm not Hera, Zeus's wife. Hera put a spell on Echo because Echo talked too much. I'm no Echo. I know how to stop talking and just walk away. Besides, Aaron isn't Narcissus. He is only trying to open my mind for answers—math answers. Aaron is not aware that my mind is a Pandora's box."

Grandma interjected. "I understand that analogy. In a way, you are like Pandora. Aaron knows about the things that Pandora had let out of the box. However, Aaron's banking on the last item that flew from the box: hope. Talking directly or indirectly using poems, class assignments, or any other words gives Aaron hope for a relationship with you."

"I never looked at things that way. I thought he was just trying to make me feel self-conscious in front of everyone at lunchtime. Then in geography class, my ego was shattered when everyone giggled at me."

"I'll be at the school meeting since your parents aren't available. I'll have ample time to size up Aaron's personality. But here's another story to think about."

"Another myth or homespun fairy tale?" Lilly asked.

"Possibly. This new tale will have enchantment, wonder, and magic. It is about choices—your choices for a career and your destiny."

"Einstein advocated reading fairy tales to children to improve their intelligence. Will this story have something about my IQ and thinking?" Lilly asked.

Grandma giggled and then answered, "Yes. Stories are important opportunities for discussing right and wrong behaviors with children. This is like my mentioning your words about Aaron in front of his peers. Feelings need to be considered. Will Rogers did say everything is funny so long as it is happening to someone else. Be careful what you say and your motive for your words."

"I understand. You've often said talking with children helps develop their conscience and basic knowledge of what is right and what is wrong. A story also provides an opportunity for critical thinking. Are you hinting that I need to be thinking more?"

"Yes, but you need to use a special type of thinking. Remember what you once said about Little Red not recognizing a wolf in her grandma's clothing?"

"I *remember*. So what is the new story?" Lilly asked.

"Your life," was the reply. "You are choosing to do too many things at one time. You aren't recognizing your energy level or paying attention to your words."

"But, Grandma, Robert Kennedy said something about some men see things. Kennedy dreamed things that never were. I too have many dreams to fulfill. Besides, I am a human Brownian motion."

"The particles in liquids and gases can be moved by light. You need to be moved with plans and schedules or else your dreams will go nowhere," Grandma responded.

"Just how can I stay focused? I have many interests and choices to consider."

"Lilly, literally cover one eye until school is out. Stop looking around for exciting adventures and challenges. And stop worrying about a career. Understanding yourself and your core strengths, like Martin Seligman recommends, hasn't helped you choose a career. Possibly, you have dual strengths that require more than one career. Relax. Enjoy your learning and growing years."

Lilly nodded her head in agreement.

"When you are with your friends, just focus on sending unique messages into space using Earth's magnetic fields. Possibly, you might include nanotechnology. And when school finishes around the end of May, uncover the covered eye. Plan the ranch for Native Americans and the active military members and their families. Even Aaron can learn and grow if he chooses to work at the ranch," Grandma said.

"I suppose latrine duty isn't that unbecoming for a volunteer to do," Lilly replied. She quickly added, "Seriously, his name would help with the new group's spelling. We'd be called A LOVE group of friends with Aaron, Lilly, Oliver, Vicky, and Ed as its members. I'll mention to the group about asking Aaron to join our club."

"I sense Aaron is getting a lot of his entertaining ideas from movies and books. His singing to you with his two pals reminds me of a movie," Grandma said.

"That's what I felt. Maverick with some buddies sang to Charlie. No doubt, the *Top Gun* movie gave Aaron ideas about singing to me at lunchtime."

"Yes, Lilly, Aaron isn't a real Maverick. Like many people, he is just copying what he has seen or read. Walk Bella, eat some vegetables, shower, and then get some rest."

"When is Mom coming home?"

"After your mother picked your sister up from band practice, they went out for supper. Because you are still healing, you need to go to bed early. Tomorrow's a new and exciting day for you. Your decision-making and knowing how to prioritize your choices needs planning. Also, think before you speak."

That night, Lilly went to bed and dreamt.

## Chapter 7A

# Change to Win


I am glad that Grandma Stormy will speak with my teachers tomorrow about my Aaron problem. I am not a fighting person. However, I wouldn't mind showing everyone just how strong I am.

I might paint the picture that's hanging in this tree. That black-and-white photograph of a horse might help me appear powerful if I were to color it with symbols. I wonder who hung this picture. Better yet, when was it hung?

Was it hung in 1493 when Columbus brought Spanish horses to North America? Or was it hung later, in 1519, when horses were reintroduced onto the North American continent?

First, I need to discover if it is a social horse or a fearful horse or an aloof horse or just a challenging one that is at the top of the pecking order. For success, I might need two personalities. I wish I might be a social and a top-of-the-pecking-order type of horse. That way, everyone would talk with me but know I was top of the pecking order.

Then, Lilly saw herself changing into two horses.

Seeing the new photograph, Lilly gasped, "No, I am becoming Mary Shelley's Frankenstein."

Bella had heard her friend cry, so she began licking Lilly's left hand. The warm and soothing touch helped Lilly center herself and her emotions.

Taking her grandma's advice, Lilly closed one eye to only see the black-and-white photograph. Still, her allergies had her thinking about using the American Bashkir Curly breed. That horse's coat, mane, tail, and inner ear hairs were curly. Indians with allergies rode that breed.

Learning from her last wish, Lilly chose to think ahead and use her words wisely. Her planned abstract art would only be for the black-and-white photograph.

Abstract art has been used by all tribes and civilizations of North and South America. It is primitive art. This art inspired 1990's art to become modern American abstract art.

Lilly wasn't thinking about using modern American but Native American art.

From a distance, students would understand her message. She wouldn't need to be careful about the words she used. Her wordless message would be painted on the horse's picture.

Nazca artwork can be seen from space. Their art covers several miles in the Peruvian desert. Lilly only needed a short distance for her message to be seen.

Planning her work, she decided not to use electroplate techniques developed in 500 AD by ancient Moche. And she wouldn't go so far as to try sand paintings like those done in ancient times.

To begin, she needed something to use to protect her skin and her horse's skin.

Lilly recalled tribes used petroleum. The oil prevented their skin from drying out. The oil also provided protection for the Indian and his horse from the biting insects. There was no available oil or sweetgrass nearby. So, like many American Indians, she chose to use a thick layer of mud.

Next, she chose her spit to mix her color powders to draw specific symbols. Those symbols would be powerful magic for herself and for her horse to become invincible. Her classmates would clearly see Lilly's courage and independence. They'd never laugh at her again. Now, where to get the colors?

The yellow color might come from flowers. Blue from berries or clays and even duck manure. The green might come from algae or moss.

Red could be made from cherries and strawberries. Red

symbolized war, blood, strength, energy, and power. Other colors had different meanings. Blue was for wisdom and confidence. Yellow meant death.

In World War I, the term yellowbelly represented a coward or a pacifist. Lilly wasn't a coward. She just didn't want to die or be laughed at. To avoid any misunderstandings, Lilly chose not to use yellow. Later, she might want to catch people with it. Yellow was her friend.

For now, possibly, she needed to use green, which had great healing powers. Her pride and ego did need mending, but she chose green to help her horse.

Better vision for her horse would happen if the circles of green were painted around the horse's eyes. Her horse did need to see where they were going.

Wait a second. Her favorite color was red; and she needed strength and power. If her horse would wear a red circle around each eye and nostril, they both would appear powerful.

Ah, but Lilly simply loved violet. Still, she didn't want to forget her favorite color, red. So, she decided to use purple—a mixture of red and blue. The blue in the purple would give her confidence to confront others.

Not thinking ahead, Lilly planned to use only one

purple upside down handprint. That symbolized a do-or-die mission.

Feeling her left hand sweating again, Lilly centered herself. She could never fight. Equally important, Lilly didn't need to prove anything to anyone.

If words and giggles and laughter came at her, she'd say to herself, "Sticks and stones might break my bones, but names and giggles and laughter could never hurt me."

Relaxing more, Lilly decided to ride her horse, her black-and-white horse, to dream land for sleep.

# Chapter 7B

# Solution

Monday was a terrific day. It began with Lilly's logical Spanish.

Then, in her second class, students were instructed to write about teens dating. "First Date" was her first article's title.

Her English teacher was prepared. Any student who finished quickly was to write another article about self-discovery.

"A Frog Rescues Lilly" was her second and longer article.

Later that morning, in her remedial math class, Lilly was given an extra assignment. Lilly was to use binary numbers for a *computer program*. The set of instructions for solving a specific problem used binary numbers for her computer to execute.

Suddenly, binary numbers were pearls, almost like the pearls Indra's god had described in a Buddhist legend. In that legend, the necklace of pearls in the heavens had one pearl reflecting other pearls.

For Lilly, artificial intelligence was a pearl for computer pearls. Program writing required showing work—binary numbers.

Smiling, Lilly glided to her art class. On her assigned wall, she hung her homework. The students were then instructed to quickly produce a second picture.

Lilly's theme was water and a boat. Surely, her teacher didn't expect an exact copy of the first picture. Her second picture would have the same theme but be focused more on the boat.

While painting, Lilly imagined the north wind as a female filling the sails with encouraging words for transporting things.

Lilly wouldn't be transporting armed men or cargo as the Vikings had. Lilly was transporting her ideas and plans for inhabiting Europa.

Vikings and Lilly had many things in common.

Each understood nature.

They were poetry lovers.

They took baths.

And they traded.

Lilly's found herself trading her love of words for her art.

As she painted the boat's watery reflection, Lilly imagined that boat on Europa, naturally, with her laptop that had newly installed programs.

After fifteen minutes, students hung their second pictures under their first ones.

"Great work, everyone. Planning several ideas is good business. Speaking of planning, I need you to think about an animal. Have some sketches for tomorrow. The animal will be for your detailed midterm project that you can also work on during your free class time. I'll speak more about it tomorrow," Mr. Brown said as the bell rang.

Earlier that same morning in the teacher's lounge, there was a discussion. Grandma Stormy requested help from two more teachers.

The science teacher, Miss French, first spoke, asking, "Should the duel be moved to different classes?"

"That might not solve anything," Coach Chuck replied. "Eventually, they would be a distraction and entertainment in other classes or in the hall and even in the lunchroom. Besides, Lilly is a good role model for other female students. She knows how to stand up for herself. Males sometimes have a commanding influence or exercise control over events, and often females allow it."

"Fine," Miss French said. "Lilly may feel insecure about her height, but she does have the ability to speak up for herself. She didn't hear Aaron's remarks today about Lilly's love needing to include him. If she had heard, I'm positive she'd have a rebuttal. Neither appears to know how to stop the duel. It's not as deadly as the Hamilton and Burr duel. Still, we don't want them to develop a long-standing bitterness."

"I understand the possible future problems," the coach said. "I will get a copy of the school's behavioral contract and add comments. Also, the two teens need to be present at the meeting. I'm still debating about attending the meeting with you. Neither Lilly nor Aaron is in any of my classes. But both want to be on the track team. That is probably why I was asked to help with the problem."

That night, Coach Chuck went to bed and dreamt.

# Chapter 8

# Now Who Is Weak?

Tossing and turning in bed that night, Coach Chuck tried to free himself from the magical powers that Lilly's yellow basket had.

Lilly had downsized a pack of animals with her yellow basket. Now she was looking at him. That picture, in his mind, haunted him.

Chuck was a new teacher. He understood teens and power struggles. In one of his educational classes, he remembered reading about not doing battle with the student unless you knew you would win.

So as far as he could see in his dream, even wild animals lost to Lilly's powerful words. If she were to team up with Aaron, for certain he'd lose.

Then, in his dream, Coach Chuck saw some of his students practicing jumping.

In another area of the track field, several students were throwing a heavy spherical object that resembled a cannonball.

Coach Chuck immediately saw Lilly and Aaron throwing a spherical-shaped dictionary with words flying at him from the dictionary's pages. Successfully ducking their words, the coach moved to another area where students were preparing for the triple and high jumps.

Everything appeared to be going just smoothly until Lilly and Aaron threw their fiberglass poles. The two were not aiming at the suspended crossbar. Their poles and words were aimed at their coach.

Even the running events had words from Lilly and Aaron. Those two were kicking their air-words at him.

That was the last word he would tolerate from the pair. He decided to send each on a three thousand mile run. But thinking ahead, he didn't want another 490 BC happening.

The 490 BC legend had Pheidippides carrying a message about victory: Niki.

But Pheidippides collapsed and died. Lilly might just be the type to run until she too collapsed and died.

The youths were literally destroying him. This would be

the end of his teaching career of only one year ... until he recalled something.

The science teacher, Miss French, would be at the meeting with the principal, the school counselor, and the student's guardian or parent. He didn't need to talk or say a word.

Soon, Chuck's attention was not about words but about Miss French.

Did she dye her hair and add red highlights to have 620 to 750 nm with a frequency of 400 to 484 THz?

Red has the lowest frequency and the longest wavelengths.

Still, those two teens he imagined as being violet waves with the shortest wave lengths. Those short waves had the most energy and would carry attack words against the tall, muscular coach.

Then, Coach Chuck wondered. Would the tiny, experienced, science teacher, Miss French, be equipped with enough skills and endurance to handle the situation?

Suddenly, the science teacher's red hair took over his thoughts and fears. She had become a new flame of hope, and he did like the color red. Red is an emotional color—not just for danger but for passion and love.

Thinking only of the lovely, beautiful teacher, he fell into a deeper sleep and smiled.

# Chapter 9

# Stay Clear and Be Safe

Absence might help the heart to grow fonder, but for Coach Chuck, absence from the meeting gave him strength. Lilly would not be able to discount or downsize that big ape of a coach.

Still, Lilly did ask for help to protect her from Aaron's words and disruptions. She needed the coach. Besides, Chuck was helping Lilly by initiating the meeting. He had sent the appropriate notes and personally telephoned guardians and families. Still, Chuck feared. Later in time, Lilly might use his words to downsize him. As a small ape, she'd be able to place the coach with the rest of the smaller pack of animals. He didn't want his dream to come true.

Safe outside the meeting room, Chuck was having fearful thoughts from his tiny imagination. Even adults have imaginations.

It wasn't until the conference group had left the principal's office smiling that the coach felt safe. Even handshakes were offered to him with words of appreciation.

"By the way, will you be willing to help Lilly rebuild her strength before track starts?"

"Gladly," the coach replied. "I need to be able to see her medical records."

"Lilly has a new physician to see tomorrow after school. May I give him your name and contact information?" Grandma Stormy asked.

"Certainly," Coach Chuck responded. Looking at the two teens, he added, "I would also like to know what your goals and interests are. Students have already begun their physical fitness exercises with me in the gym. Anytime you two are ready, come join us in the gym before and after school. I'm even available on Saturday mornings for helping you practice."

Miss French smiled.

That made Coach Chuck smile back.

He continued smiling the whole day, while Lilly planned her art and her words.

# Chapter 10

## Science Fiction Contest

After school that same day, Lilly felt safe and at peace with the world. With less stress from Aaron, Lilly had energy to enter a writing competition.

To enter the contest, a few pages needed to be submitted. And if Lilly won the contest, she'd be given a cash prize. That money would be used for the summer's ranch. She might even enjoy reading her winning novel to children who were interested in science and not necessarily numbers.

Thus, Lilly chose color words instead of frequency numbers.

The 4HTz would be called Red. The 4.5HTz would be called Orange, and 5HTz would be named Yellow.

The 6HTz would represent Green, closely related to the 6.5HTz for Blue. Violet would be 7HTz.

Any interested reader, or science enthusiast, could Google for exact numbers. Her story needed other characters.

An independent thinker would be named Tac.

A wise person would be called Sofia.

Thinking about binary numbers for program writing, Lilly added Zoe from a planet world named Zero One to Infinity.

The plot would be to bring Dream back to life and rescue Earth from harmful radiation (Violet) and selfish love (Cupid).

Lilly chose to be the heroine—the person who acted with extraordinary courage.

*Rescue Mission* was the title for her novel.

*****

## Rescue Mission

The 007 Cosmos Bond container was full. The inhalator had finished topping it with CQD and SOS signals from Earth.

As early as 1905, messages had been thrown from Earth.

Then, in 1906, the International Radiotelegraphic Convention in Berlin finally chose ... --- ... (or SOS) instead of the CQD signals. The crew was not aware of the happening.

Icebergs were disappearing on Earth. The Titanic did hit an iceberg.

Possibly, one signal was from the Titanic, and the other was from the iceberg that used a different code.

Knowledgeable Tac explained to the colors that the Captain on the Titanic was from the UK, so he used the CQD signal to call for help.

A youth on the Titanic was aware of the new established universal SOS signal, so he used the SOS signal to call for help.

"That explains the double signals from the Titanic. But what can explain the two gold discs that we also retrieved?" Orange asked.

Tac noted, "Gold has been a precious metal on Earth."

"Yes," Yellow added. "They probably have some fellow like Midas change other elements into gold. Gold isn't as precious to the inhabitants. Now, they are just throwing it away."

"I am more interested in the messages with several foreign languages recorded on those two gold records. Are they bragging or asking for help?" Red asked.

"Earth must be a foolish planet. That planet has a lot of wealth and natural resources. The inhabitants are just wasting their resources and their words," Green said.

"For this dimension in space tunneling, we will need to return to our planet, Zero One to Infinity. There, I can use our computers programed with binary numbers," Zoe said. "We do not deal with time. However, what we've collected might be in some different order of happenings."

Tac prepared the next instrument for use. It was necessary to install the harmonic resonance frequency that would manipulate matter and sound at the atomic level.

On Earth, a Serbian American inventor and scientist, Nikola Tesla, had proposed harmonic resonance frequency technology.

Using Tesla's technology, they returned to their Zero One to Infinity world.

In snap time, back on their planet, the rainbow unformed into ROYGBIV, single colors. Their rainbow wasn't the aboriginal rainbow that uses its energy and breath to give people life. Their rainbow was like several rainbow galaxies with fingerprints identifiable on Earth as empathy.

In a twinkle of light, the borrowed 101 Cosmo Container from another universe had every piece of information categorized. It was simple to understand the basis for the messages. The denominator was fear.

Suggestions were then submitted by the color frequencies beginning with the lowest power rank and ending with the highest power rank speaking.

Red suggested freezing neurons of the PFC that oscillate at 4 hertz. This would reduce fear responses for the Earth people.

Orange disagreed. "Go directly to the neurons of the

BLA. That part of their brain would be best used for eliminating their fears."

Yellow beamed a relaxed 5 and said, "The process is driven by the PFC. Why waste energy going elsewhere? They need to experience theta waves from 3 to 8 hertz to relax—deeply relax. In their relaxed minds, we can provide needed mental imagery for overriding their fears. If they haven't mastered their thinking habits by now, we might need them to use fasting. Fasting changes the brain."

The next higher up ranking frequency, Green, agreed.

Blue was on call. His heightened attention and wisdom were needed to address the sudden detected gravitational waves.

Gravitational waves, at the speed of light, were causing another 1,001 Cosmos Container to extend in one direction. Its unclassified contents were moving in a perpendicular direction.

The new incoming messages, requiring help, were in their dimension of events—their time concepts.

In the past folds of existence, Titan had never required help or hope from the rainbow group of colors. The inhabitants only forwarded signals of gratitude.

The gratitude came from all walks of life, for every

breath produced on Titan. Appreciation came from all points on the 1,600-mile radius of that moon.

The Cosmos is 250 times larger than the visible universe. Still, wherever life existed, their feelings vibrated on the same frequency. This is a fact that all types of rainbows know.

Knowledge, however, is at a different frequency. For example, the pursuit of a lifestyle or daily bread means different things, even though people vibrate at the same frequency.

Knowledge is a game changer.

Once, French queen Marie Antoinette had heard her peasants had no bread. She had no knowledge about the conditions and daily struggles of her people.

"Let them eat cake," Marie Antoinette suggested.

Basically, it was brioche, which is almost as rich as cake. The queen lacked knowledge about her people's hardships.

Some advisor needed to explain the basic needs of her people. Then, the queen might have developed a love feeling, a 639 Hz, which is also a frequency of connection.

Now, at the ninth dimension, there were no explanations for Tac and Zoe doing things together without including

Violet. No one had explained anything to Violet. There was a connection, but it didn't include Violet.

Violet's feelings were hurt. Her hurt became her anger, which she hid with a smile.

Like with the queen, no one had taken time to explain to Violet how she might connect with others. Thus, Violet chose never to be in a rainbow or in the same light with independent-thinking Tac and planning ahead with binary-number Zoe.

To magnify the situation, Violet also chose to change. She transformed herself into infrared light. She believed no one would ever see her.

But an international group of scientists from Poland, Switzerland, Norway, and the United States had discovered certain conditions that made the infrared light visible.

Now, being angry might cause a person to see red is a scientific fact.

Being jealous is normal, but Violet didn't see red; instead, she becomes infrared energy.

By the way, astronomers divide infrared into near-infrared (0.75 microns) midinfrared (5 to 30 microns) and far-infrared (30 to 1000 microns).

Basically, infrared energy isn't dangerous unless narrowed into a beam of very high power.

And Violet had become thin-skinned—narrow to the core.

Any good mirror is capable of reflecting infrared light, unless jealousy angled it.

Now, don't get infrared (Violet) wrong. There are uses for infrared radiation.

The infrared camera is used to find people in burning, smoke-filled buildings. The military uses it to inspect electrical systems, navigate, study oceanography, and other things.

So, relaxing with positive thinking, Violet, now called Infrared, chose to be useful—a true and helpful Infrared.

Soon, she came out of hiding and became her true self, Violet. Violet even rejoined her rainbow group of friends. Rainbows make people happy because rainbows symbolize hope and a promise of sunshine. Violet enjoyed making people happy.

Still, being somewhat human, Violet wanted to be with other groups. She also desired other friends to do different things besides making people happy and giving hope.

But the truth was Violet didn't enjoy being last in her rainbow group of friends. Violet was not aware of her strength and beauty when she was with the right group of friends.

Sadly, Violet hadn't been careful about selecting a new friend. And, so it was that when Violet and Cupid became friends, they began gossiping and judging others and excluding others in many ways.

In the past, when not on call with the rainbow group, Violet had Dream as her closest friend.

In Violet's thinking, Dream was a bit like gamma rays that are used to treat cancer. Violet felt Dream would help her reputation. Violet was falling in love with Dream.

At one moment in time, Violet discovered some scary information. Gamma ray bursts were used to study things about the solar system, galaxies, and the whole universe. So, she devised a plan to keep her Dream on Earth with her.

That is why Violet encouraged Dream to be successful on Earth. Thus, it was with a new infant's cry, centered at 3,500 HTz, Dream interjected a purpose and wish to live.

The normal resting heartbeat of a newborn infant is between 100 to 150 beats per minute. It is at the intervals when there is no heartbeat when Dream wove in hope. Hope was in the form of optimism or 2 to 432 Hz frequency energy.

Even adults could use Dream for enhancing creativity, problem-solving, and finding insights into their well-being.

Naturally, Dream became busy. He forgot about being

Violet's boyfriend. Dream was able to work alone in the dark.

In the blink of an eye, there was a gravitational wave. Yes, that was the exact fold in time when Violet and Cupid had become friends.

That was the exact fold in time that blocked all life from having a dream. Suddenly, without a job, Dream was alone and without a purpose in life. Naturally, Dream sought his old friend Violet, but he couldn't find her.

When Dream didn't give Violet the attention she needed, Violet became upset. Dream had never realized not only was he important for newborns' futures but for adults' daily confidence.

To amplify matters, Cupid and Violet began acting like two black holes. They collided to send small but detectable gravitational waves that blocked Dream from ever existing. The pair became Dream killers.

Hearing about Cupid and Violet destroying Dream, Tac devised a plan to empower one specific female to return Dream to all ages of life.

"The female will have empathy and super strength to hold Dream in her arms and bring him back to life. That child shall be named Lilly," Sofia announced.

"To keep Lilly safe, she must have a dog that has an extra sense of the child's thinking and feeling," Tac suggested.

"Our readings in this splash of future time show the girl named Lilly is now fourteen, and Dream is still dead," Green informed everyone.

"Will that beanpole be willing to use her extraordinary courage and have enough focus to bring Dream back to life? Or will she spend her entire life grieving and thinking only of her loss?" Orange asked.

Wise Sofia assured everyone that Lilly would stay focused and not go off the path like Little Red Riding Hood had done. Lilly would help Earth by first changing her loss into a gift."

Sofia was unaware of a dog grabbing Cupid's whole note from Cupid's pouch. Who had sent the dog to steal love's enduring powers?

*****

That was all Lilly wrote for the science fiction contest. Only a few pages were required to enter the contest.

Quickly, she emailed a copy to the contest's publisher.

"I love you, Bella," Lilly sighed. "I hope I can understand my father's sudden death and Mom quickly remarrying by writing about it. Somehow, I will make the loss a gift in order to move forward and help Earth. Possibly, my fear of masculine muscles will save our Earth."

Bella yawned.

Lilly's restless legs syndrome and talking while dreaming helped Bella detect Lilly's panic attacks and the need to lick Lilly's left hand. Bella could even see Lilly's sweat. Also, when Lilly was asleep or awake, the dog had learned to detect smells, movements, and body postures to know if Lilly was nervous, anxious, or afraid.

Patting her friend's head, Lilly softly spoke, "This writing contest is easier for me to do than creating another worm as I had done in sixth grade. Now I wonder how my novel will proceed?"

Lilly yawned. She then recalled her parents' words in their den the week before school had started.

Her parents reminded Lilly of two caring love birds or beautiful swans.

She and Bella were soon relaxed on the Lilly's bed.

That night, Lilly dreamt.

# Chapter 11

# Adult Conversations

Bella and Cuddles were the only witnesses. Their newly sharpened seeing and hearing experienced two adults.

"I am not getting any younger, darling," David said. "We could use the extra money for our daughters' college education. Please, reconsider my wanting to leave the navy and work for the Academia, previously known as Blackwater. Eric was a former Navy SEAL officer who started the company. The assignment would help the International Space Station collect orbital debris."

"That's a risky job, darling," Sunny uttered. "Orbital debris is junk from launched objects."

"The debris is in low Earth orbit areas where the Space Station flies. The task of retrieving space junk is very exciting," David reported. "I'll be safe using a space harpoon instead of a giant butterfly net to clean up seven thousand tons of trash."

"David, think for a second. The space junk can move 4.3 to five miles per second. That speed is seven times faster than a bullet fired from a gun. What about going into politics? You have a good history background," Sunny suggested.

"You're right. I do know history as well anyone else interested in the subject. Many Navy men became presidents. John F. Kennedy, Lyndon Johnson, Richard Nixon, Gerald Ford, Jimmy Carter—all had served in the Navy as well as George H. W. Bush. But my favorite president was an optimist. He was an air force man."

"I remember you mentioning reading Reagan's memoir. You agreed with his committing American troops only as a last resort," Sunny noted.

Smiling, David walked slowly, like a confident tiger, closer and closer to his wife. "I love and care for you very much. Your safety is my concern. Please think. Your choice just ..."

David had begun hugging and kissing his wife. David's first love was adventure on land, in the water, and now in the new frontier—space.

David was not the talking type. Why should he explain things?

They loved each other, and nothing else mattered. Wasn't that how a marriage worked?

Violet and Cupid had placed a wedge between the couple that was in the form of not being a team with decisions. Violet and Cupid also planned to split nations and their leaders, so they'd never work together.

But three hours earlier, David had signed a contract. Unlike David's signature, Lilly's hand was wet.

Noticing Lilly's anxiety, Bella had begun licking Lilly's left hand.

*****

Sitting straight up in bed, Lilly thought, I was dreaming. I don't think my parents need to be in my science fiction novel. My dad doesn't need to pick up rainbow messages or the gold ring on the dog's collar.

As if agreeing, Bella again yawned.

I'll spare myself worries by not including my family in my science fiction, but I feel ideas about my parents' courtship might be in the play this summer at the ranch. Just what would that play need besides performers and costumes? Why, a setting and a plot are needed.

Giggling, Lilly thought of a ranch. It needed cowboys, cowgirls, cows, and horses.

When they were in grade school, Aaron had once mentioned to Lilly that he wanted to ride a horse, even perform in a rodeo.

The summer play at the ranch might be about an older man falling in love with a young girl, something like her mother, Sunny, and father, Jim, had done.

I believe my new dad, David, is also older than mom. I'll marry an older man, Lilly thought. My ideas for the summer ranch performance need this type of romantic love.

Lilly was certain that if Rudyard Kipling knew Lilly, Kipling would like the rodeo and not another jungle setting.

Then, Lilly remembered the LOVE group would be meeting to discuss methods for sending their messages into space. Lilly would propose using the Earth's core.

Suddenly, Lilly realized the Earth's resonance might be used as a global thermometer, a clue to when magnetic pole shifting would happen. This knowledge would help prepare airports and failed energy grids and even satellites for mass blackouts.

For the time being, Lilly needed to get some sleep, but

there were so many things she wanted to do. Would she have the time and the energy to do everything? Falling asleep, Lilly remembered Davenport Babcock's poem, "Be Strong."

# Chapter 12

# A Wise Art Teacher

Lilly's fourth class was art. In her dream the night before, her new dad chose to remain silent about a choice he had already made. Lilly chose to do the same. Who would be the wiser one to know?

Lilly decided to use a last year's drawing for the midterm. Besides saving time, she just loved birds. That was what she told herself. Lilly needed time to think about her science fiction novel, so why not use one of her beloved birds?

Lilly giggled. She was so full of herself.

Mr. Brown knew about Lilly's past and especially about her love for birds. Mr. Brown was also a bird lover.

To help Lilly develop new talents, Mr. Brown would not allow any birds.

To avoid routine art, he also omitted fish and another student's past work.

Still, Lilly wanted to use a bird running, possibly from reality called honesty. For the moment, that picture rested in her art folder with a few sketches of a dog, kola bears, and a still life scene for her science fiction novel.

Aristotle's *Nicomachean Ethics* noted that no one does wrong willingly but only out of ignorance of the consequences of their actions. Plato felt people did wrong things because things were pleasurable for the moment. Others might believe they were excused from the consequences of their actions. Ignorance or pleasure should not inhibit one's ability to make the right choice. Good things always outweigh the pain or discomfort in doing them.

The class, busy with practices and demonstrations, quickly ended. Lilly's past stayed in her art portfolio and not in her mind.

The next day, after taking attendance, the art class was told to view pictures that had been taken from space.

"Next week, I'll explain the two lists, showing my sketched birds that are hanging on the door.

I love birds, and I always sketch some with information for your notes. One of my goals is to have you develop your talents using your ever-changing skills and knowledge."

Lilly felt shame for planning to use last year's bird. Her teacher was trying to develop her talents. The new knowledge had her deciding not to use last year's art. Her life was a journey and had learning and growing opportunities to use values as her guideposts.

Then, she heard her teacher speaking. "Look at the slides shown on the smart screen. They were taken in space by astronauts."

Lilly leaned forward in her chair with excitement and desert plans. This was an opportunity to explain how the desert could come alive with people and vegetation using her grandmother's suggestion and Vicky's cloud ideas.

"One astronaut taking the pictures might have been Lilly's dad."

Smiling, Lilly felt it was very thoughtful of her teacher to mention her dad.

"Your geography teacher wants you to see the connection between North America and the other six continents. Mr. Hill is sharing his slides to explain the lithosphere with its plate tectonics."

Hearing plate tectonics, Lilly suddenly thought of Oliver's statement: "Possibly, like Earth, Europa had plate tectonics under their slabs of ice. Places on those plates might provide and support living conditions for people."

Then Lilly heard her teacher say, "I am using the slides while introducing the three primary colors: red, yellow, and blue."

One picture continued to speak to Lilly's imagination.

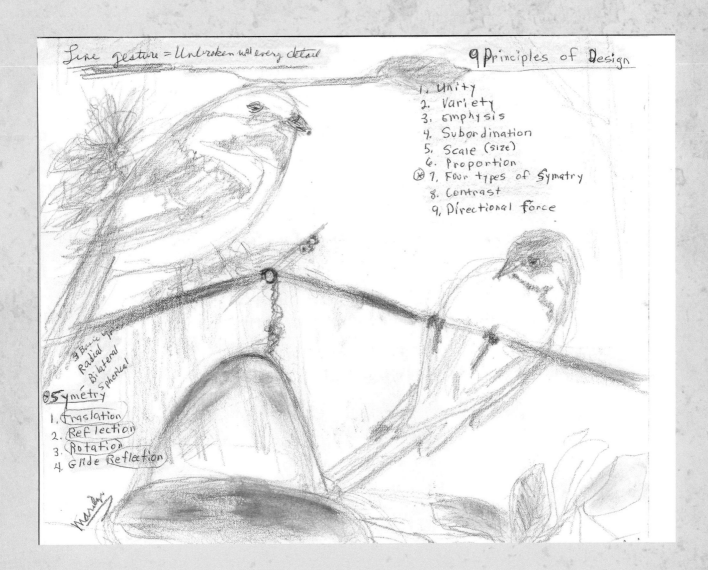

Line gesture = Unbroken w/l every detail

9 Principles of Design

1. Unity
2. Variety
3. Emphysis
4. Subordination
5. Scale (size)
6. Proportion
⊛ 7. Four types of Symatry
8. Contrast
9. Directional force

3 Basic types
Radial
Bilateral
Spherical

⊛ Symétry
1. Traslation
2. Reflection
3. Rotation
4. Glide Reflection

"By the way, what you see may not be what others or what I see due to our different perceptions, beliefs, and eyes."

If only her teacher would stop talking. Lilly was anxious to begin sketching.

"Monet was the founder of French Impressionist painting. He rejected the traditional approach to painting landscapes. Monet couldn't see blue, possibly due to cataracts. In 1923, Monet had surgery on his left eye. Thereafter, he began using special green glasses and did not undergo surgery for his other eye."

Looking directly at some students who were wearing glasses, he commented, "Shortsighted eyes are better at seeing *long* wavelengths, like red. Long-sighted eyes see the *short* wavelengths clearer, like green and blue colors."

Then, holding up a copy of another artist's work, he told the students to think about self-taught Dutch artist Vincent van Gogh and his color choices.

"Now, select two slides to copy. Begin, like the Dutch artist, by using charcoal to quickly define the negative and positive spaces. Then select *one* or several of the three primary colors to finish your work."

That was exactly what Lilly was doing using the soft, friable, brown charcoal made at 572 degrees F (300 C).

The Sahara Desert, located in northern Africa, has temperatures soaring to 117 degrees F (47 C). But that slide had Lilly only seeing sand, not heat. Her imagination directed her sketching to using brown charcoal for creating the desert's sand.

Soon, her pigments changed the brown charcoal drifts of sand into colors for grass, plants, and trees. Her finished picture did not look like the original monochromatic brown desert.

Lilly's imagination saw people living and working in deserts—that is, after liquid clay was sprayed onto the sand. Using liquid clay nanoparticles encourages fungus to live and help plant roots use the nitrates, or fertilizers.

For her second choice, Lilly tried to be an Impressionist like the French painter Eugene Henri Paul Gauguin.

Gauguin had no restraints as to what art needed to be. He worked beyond imagination. He even influenced Pablo Picasso. Gauguin had been Vincent van Gogh's friend, and both were in the Postimpressionism movement. Her teacher certainly wanted the style, not the artist's color choices, so she thought. Or was that what she thought she had heard?

For her second slide's choice, Lilly's imagination was doing a duel with Gauguin's imagination. She was re-creating French Polynesian art for the slide that showed the world's busiest ports located on the Yangtze River delta.

After placing her two-colored sketches on the class work table, she heard her teacher.

"Next week, I'll hang your work on the ceiling with numbers instead of your names. You'll match the number with the artist. It will be an opportunity to know your peers, not by their name but by their art."

The remainder of the class time, students worked on their homework, drawing their future careers with animals. The animal needed to be different than the midterm's choice. For that quarter, they were focusing on animals.

# Chapter 13

# Career

The following day, each student hung his or her assignment for evaluation. *Dependent* was the emotional word Lilly had written on the back of her work with Cherney for music.

Lilly's journal had sketches and splashes of color for her testing hue, tint, tone, and shade. She felt each picture needed a word on the back.

If she ever sold her work, the information on the picture's back could be quickly referred to instead of paging through her journal.

That assignment had Lilly finally committed to art as her future career.

Still, she might change her mind.

87

Julia Child wrote her first cookbook when she was fifty. Henry Ford was forty-five years old when he made the Model T car. Harry Bernstein finally got a hit when he was ninety-six. Grandma Moses began painting prolifically at seventy-eight.

Plato did say something about inventions having a mother named necessity. And Earth's weather did need help. Lilly often changed her mind.

Suddenly, hearing comments from other students, especially statements about her work, pulled Lilly back to Earth.

By mistake, Lilly had also hung a watercolor intended for the science fiction contest that had Violet and Cupid hiding in her art.

Mr. Brown smiled and said, "Well done, everyone. Would anyone like to explain their planned career and color choices?"

Lilly raised her hand and spoke, "By mistake, I had hung a colored still life. That's for a science fiction contest, and it's hiding Cupid and Violet. For today's assignment, I'm using the gray kolas on one of my trade's tools."

Looking directly at her teacher, she continued. "I realize gray is a cool, neutral, balanced color. Gray represents intelligence. I know who I am and what I can achieve. I am independent when it comes to my career choice: a watercolor artist. Later in time, I will use violet. Violet is for the future, for my imagination and writings."

Other students explained their works and color choices.

"Change today's assignment into a marketable product. Remember," Mr. Brown continued, "be cost effective. Include any needed written directions for assembling the profitable product."

Without hesitation, Lilly began resketching.

Lilly had felt frightened hearing talk about dangers with espionage, 18 US Code Ch 37.

Thinking of and designing a marketable product developed from a fear would be a positive way for her to heal. Soon, Lilly began producing ideas for a bookmark and note cards. The assignment wasn't due until the following week. However, Lilly's imagination and the reader's eyes can see the finished product before next week on the following page.

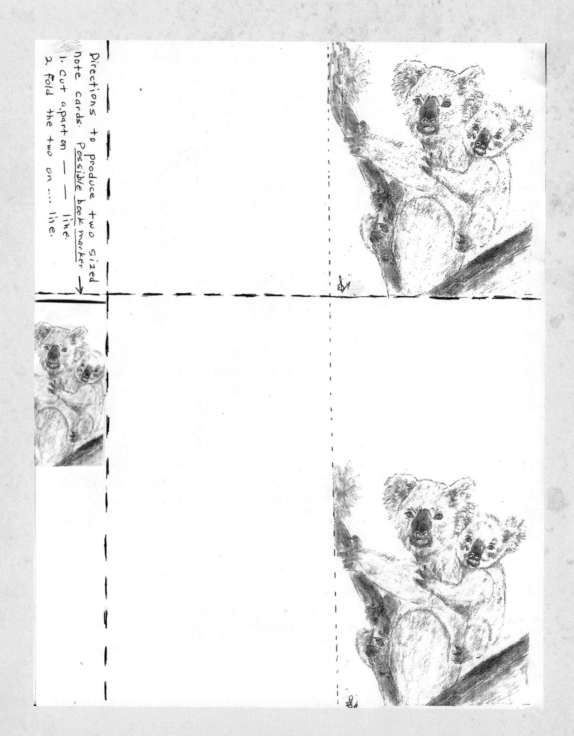

Directions to produce two sized
note cards. Possible book marker
1. Cut apart on — — line.
2. Fold the two on ··· line.

90

# Chapter 14

# Women Also Have Testosterone

One might believe a male hormone was only for men. That isn't exact._A female's ovaries not only produce estrogen but also small amounts of testosterone.

Another gland that produces hormones is the thyroid. Those hormones are for metabolism and growth. The small thyroid is located below the skin and muscle fat in the front of the neck. It is brownish red in color and weighs only an ounce. If one did not know better, he might see his thyroid and say, "I have a butterfly in my neck."

Lilly had grown taller and faster than her peers. Her new physician had assured everyone that Lilly had no thyroid problems, and she wouldn't have gigantism. As far as her mono condition, Lilly now was healthy. She did need to regain muscle strength.

Lilly wasn't moving about not because she was ill but because she had become lazy. Sometimes, writing and drawing were easier to do than using her energy for exercise.

Energy can come from many sources. For Lilly, her energy came from praises. Lilly lived for encouraging words. Her art and English teachers were not stingy with giving students kudos.

In the past, her parents often said, "Lilly, we truly love you." Possibly one more time would help.

"We are always available for you and anxious to hear whatever is on your mind."

That last statement was no doubt true—at one time, that is. But now Sunny was busy. Her part-time job and studying for her GED used her energy. And her dad wasn't around to talk with. He was away for special training.

Lilly was a beautiful woman, and she knew it. And, equally important, Lilly was a female with testosterone.

A picture is needed, not words.

Now, Mary Howitt might have a spider using flattering words to catch a fly in the poem, "The Spider and the Fly." But one female in a battle was using words to break free and become independent. The teen's words weren't flattering.

In any event, horns or words were locked in a battle. One deeply wounded another with piercing, angry words.

Motherhood is more than a physical happening. It can be a loss of self for the betterment and survival of the child. In return, respect was all that Sunny requested.

Conflict had begun when Sunny wanted her daughter to exercise and not talk about dating an older man. But like in a Slavonic rhapsody, there was a sudden burst, and it wasn't into a dance. The perfect listener, the mother, simply said, "No," to dating Amor.

It began like a melody of romantic love, and then quickly and abruptly, the rhythm changed. Lilly was not mature enough to assert herself without dominating her mother. Once more, Lilly was talking without thinking.

Amor might have been older than Lilly, but Lilly believed in eight types of Greek love—exactly which type, no one knows. Not letting her date certainly didn't reflect her mother's love for her. Besides, Lilly was a certified know-it-all. She even had an advanced degree in knowing everything because she had more education than her mother.

To add to Lilly's problem, she had realized her present physical appearance attracted males. Would developing her muscles cause males to find her less attractive? Exercise just might overdevelop her muscles. Lilly certainly didn't want to take any chances.

Earlier that Friday night, Lilly had proven she was the master of the rigorous mental game of chess. She was aggressive and a powerhouse over the board and others playing against her. She would never win if she played against Judit Polgár, the strongest female chess player of all time.

Still, opponents feared being matched against Lilly. Some even went so far as to leave the area when they saw her. But Amor appeared to be drawn to her strength. Or was it her beauty … or her age? Or was it love?

White on the chessboard moves first. And that's just what Lilly did when she saw the dusty, sun-tanned, lanky cowboy smile at her.

Lilly smiled back, a smile without restraints or braces. And that is exactly what Lilly and her mother talked about using words without pictures. Really!

Earlier that day, Amor and Lilly had met at a chess tournament. Lilly had just sacrificed her queen, which was a queenside pawn, to speed things up in the game. The queen's gambit had positions on the board equal, or just about equal.

Several endgame strategies might have taken place, but Lilly used her queen and her pawn to box off the escape routes for the opponent's king.

Winning, Lilly used her Cassian smile and looked up. Naturally, Cupid and Violet were watching as Lilly carelessly walked into Cupid's arrows that had violet feathers.

How could such a carless thing happen? Amor had just been standing behind Lilly's opponent and was minding his own business, or was he just minding his own business? But, man, he was cute. And that was just it—a man had paid attention to Lilly.

Winning the tournament was an emotion that saw an almost familiar-looking man—in many ways like her deceased father, Jim.

And just what had happened to one with twenty-five more years of knowledge and experience and one now just fourteen?

Paul Cézanne really knew Lilly. Cezanne believed emotion began art. Or was it that emotion began love? Anyway, the emotion with winning and suddenly seeing a father figure had Cupid jumping for joy.

Lilly's mother, Sunny, had just turned sixteen when she met Jim, a strong, handsome sailor. Jim had swept the teen to distant shores and to meeting Lilly.

Sunny tried to reason with her daughter, saying that being sixteen is two years older than fourteen. But Lilly didn't understand the math. Lilly's present actions showed Lilly would never outsmart a rat.

But wait, rats are intelligent. Rats can navigate and remember their routes.

If Lilly needed attention, well, let it be known rats also need attention. Rats even enjoy being tickled. And, after making love, a male rat uses 20 to 22 kHz. Lilly used to be like a rat. Both showed empathy. Both could understand another's pain.

But now, Lilly just shouted without feeling her mother's pain leaking out as tears.

"And that Amor … Just what does he do for a living?" her mother had asked.

Don't be quick to judge Amor. Amor had not been aware of Lilly's age. Also, Sunny needed to be careful using loud words. Some young hearts only want a carefree dance to their own tunes and possibly be like their mothers.

Parenting and discipline require guidance, not shouting.

Anyway, Lilly mentioned riding broncos, roping calves, wrestling steers, and earning rodeo champion belt buckles. It was a respectable career.

The next day was Saturday, and at sunset, no rodeo clowns were seated in the living room to distract a charging youth's need for attention and independence. No, not even one clown was present to relieve the tension and change panic to a calm frequency. And no one was humming classical music to relax the atmosphere.

There was only a family and one guest for dinner. And wouldn't parents want their children to be like them? Didn't Sunny see what her daughter saw—a father figure?

Age was never mentioned. Let's be honest. Math is not always the universal language for emotions. Going into adulthood didn't need mentioning. Why make wild guesses about anyone's maturity?

Topics David quietly mentioned included economics, religion, and preparation classes for marriage in their church. Finally, David spoke about knowing their life's goals and dreams—with a career and a budget in mind. Independent people are just that, independent.

Amor and Lilly quietly sat. They were good listeners.

"Basically," Amor said, "I became interested in discovering how Lilly knew so many different moves on the gameboard with sixty-four squares arranged in an eight-by-eight grid. Her timing was amazing. When she looked at me and invited me over for dinner at her home, I thought I was going to her home—I mean, her home, not her family's."

Lilly had never noticed the man when she was changing locations to play other opponents. Just where had Amor been before her last winning game? Lilly suddenly questioned just what the older man was doing at the tournament? Why was he following her from one opponent to another? Amor didn't appear to know anything about the game—the game of chess, that is.

Lilly was also amazed that she had never noticed the scars on Amor's left cheek, upper lip, and left hand. His fingernails needed filing and cleaning.

And to think that she had intended to hug and kiss him. Just what had she been thinking? Was she too busy listening to his exciting rodeo stories to really notice details about his scars and grime?

As Amor exited, he mentioned something about needing some shut-eye to be able to get an early start for the next rodeo in another state with two of his buddies who were waiting for him in their car that was parked outside Lilly's home.

After the door had closed, Lilly collapsed into her dad's arms. Believe you me, Sunny wanted to do the same thing.

Finally, Lilly spoke. "Dad, your composure deserves a medal of honor. From the bottom of my heart and to the top of my future, I want to say thank you for being calm and useful with your words. You saved me from making some horrible mistakes.

"Mom, I am so very sorry for arguing with you. Please, Mom, forgive me. I not only was wrong but disrespectful. Please forgive me."

"Yes, Lilly, I forgive you. When I didn't give you attention immediately, it was for a reason. Now, let's eat. Vicky is probably very hungry, having had to listen to the conversations with the smells of food, now banquet food, near her in the kitchen."

Lilly smelled the food. Banquet or not, she was hungry.

In that moment, it was almost like a clear, cool Thanksgiving Day with no visible clouds in the sky. There were no low stratus clouds, no cumulus clouds, no cirrus clouds, and no nimbus clouds in sight.

However, if one were to look closely, two protective panda clouds might be seen in the sunset's yellow and settled-red sky.

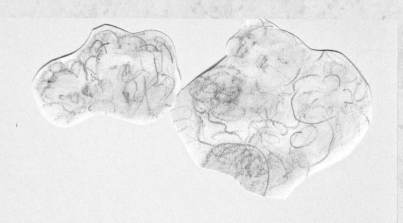

# Chapter 15

# Plans

After eating and again apologizing to her mother, Lilly went to her room. She began writing ideas for the characters in the play at the ranch during the coming summer. She wanted her play to be used.

She chose Amor to be played by Aaron. Why not write about her almost mistake and make the whole thing a comedy?

Had Lilly's common sense hidden from her again? Why pull Aaron into an almost tragic mistake? Besides, Aaron might not want to have Lilly as a director. Lilly was planning a life for herself and friends to be captive in her attic needs.

Besides that, Lilly really didn't have time to write the play, complete her science fiction story, and do her class assignments. The group needed to write the play.

Then Lilly wondered why Aaron wasn't at the chess tournament. Suddenly, Lilly realized Aaron was staying away due to the conference meeting. At the school meeting, Lilly had requested Aaron stay away from her. She also wanted to figure out how many things she was capable of being committed to doing. She was old enough to be responsible for her schedule.

Hurrying back into the kitchen to speak with her dad, she heard him ask, "What took you so long to figure things out?"

"I didn't have the words to express myself. I now know what a family's *enduring love* means. That's *true love*."

After a few more grateful hugs and thanks, Lilly went back to her room to work on her science fiction novel. Lilly continued to develop the plot to include strengths and weaknesses for Violet and Cupid. The full note, which was now on a dog's collar, was the clue for her loss becoming a gift.

**The whole note on the dog's collar needed to be hidden from Cupid. Cupid had plans to wave that whole note at unprepared teens. The dog must be captured at all costs before Cupid could ruin lives.**

**But first, Violet would attempt getting inside Lilly's mind. The teen needed foolish dreams with false hopes. That would be the only way the whole note could work.**

**This wouldn't be easy unless Lilly permitted others to lead her life with their schedules and their dreams. Lilly had been choosing friends wisely. So, Violet and Cupid would need to use brute force on Lilly. But what might they use? They certainly didn't want her to develop her**

muscles and be strong enough and focused in order to bring Dream back to life.

Thus, they chose a feather to tickle the teen's imagination into believing independence would provide true happiness and tranquility for an unprotected, untrained, immature teenager.

*****

**The feather would only work if Lilly's courage and schedules were weakened.**

**To weaken Lilly, Violet, with Cupid's help, had to annihilate and destroy Lilly's common sense and hide the teen's true reason for bringing Dream back to life.**

*****

Thinking of her new work schedule, Lilly emailed a copy to her future publisher with a note saying there was more to follow during her Christmas break. Lilly had been selected as one of the three finalists.

Lilly thought to herself, *I suppose males do like females with muscles. If not, I will exercise in moderation. My parents just want me to be healthy. I'll ask Coach Chuck just what I need to work on to be strong enough for three track events.* Then, stretching to the sky, she decided to mention to her coach her fear of too many muscles.

Hearing Bella yawn, Lilly looked down and said, "Sorry, dear friend. I won't be drawing you for the writing contest. I will, however, begin sketching you tomorrow for the midterm art project. By the way, my English teacher, with my parents' approval, has submitted the two short article I wrote in class for publication."

Smiling, Lilly continued explaining things to Bella. "One article was sent to *Families and Friends* magazine. The second article was sent to a magazine titled *Journey for Understanding the Self.* I thought my art project, bookmark, and note cards were money makers. It appears my words are profitable as well. I wonder if this is my dual career."

As Lilly headed outside to walk Bella for the evening, both stopped to gaze into the night sky.

Venus could be seen before sunset but now appeared to be shining on Lilly. Possibly, Venus, the only planet named after a goddess, was trying to praise another female.

Mercury was also visible and no doubt chose to recognize Lilly. Mercury was the first and primary planet of intelligence.

Then, Lilly thought about her magazine articles. One was about her fear of too many muscles in "A Frog Rescues Lilly." But thinking about her first published article, titled "First Date," had Lilly hugging her dog.

# Chapter 16

# Lilly's Two Magazine Stories

*First Date: Introduction*

Lilly and Vicky's parents finally gave their approval for their daughters to date in a group.

The parents felt the girls, staying together, would be safe to explore relationships by dating in a group. All the planning, discussing, and information did not include a race to be the first car to cross the ice-covered bridge.

Often, a drowning person sees her life passing before her eyes. This might explain Lilly's giggle then gurgle then seeing her parents' military wedding.

*First Date*

    *Lilly and her sister's first date had been a group date.*
    *When a person is drowning, her life flashes before her eyes. Her life and expectations for her future are vividly imagined.*
    *The first picture that Lilly saw was her parents' wedding. Lilly finally understood why her mother had remarried.*

The second image that Lilly saw was her doing experiments in a medical lab on Europa. The third image was Vicky writing music with healing frequencies for Earth's weather.

Sadly, Lilly did not see two Nobel Prizes. One was for her medical discovery. The second was for her sister's music, which healed Earth's weather.

Those two Nobel Prizes might have been in the future—a future she and her sister would never have.

It all began when Lilly and Vicky's parents had discussions and talks about dress codes, acting codes, thinking codes, and seat belts codes. All talks forgot to include group behavior while driving down a rode that led over an icy bridge.

The right eye tears first when one cries for happiness, and both eyes tear for pain. More than a dozen pairs of eyes teared that evening.

Before tears, there was giggling, more giggling, and then gurgling sounds. Lilly would suddenly see her military wedding—a wedding she wanted but would never experience.

Other pictures and thoughts followed until there were two teen-sized coffins and a third, just the right size for Bella.

Yes, two cars had raced over a bridge in a competition to challenge different vehicles. One dog had raced on a bridge covered in patches of snow to help two floating in icy waters.

Note: For the published magazine article, the names of the children and dog were changed.

A Frog Rescues Lilly

In someone else's story, the kissed frog would turn into a prince. A fairy tale like that would prevent Lilly from maturing and grow up with reality.

There, however, is another type of frog—a frogman now called a Navy SEAL. Lilly's stepdad is a green-faced SEAL.

David gave his stepdaughter a gift—his Sioux family's medicine woman. Not many people realize each Indian Nation had healers who began training at an early age.

A child would be identified and guided to learning about healing plants, trees, roots, berries, and other foods used, as well as learn songs and prayers. The number of days a child would fast differed for each chosen child. Training age was equally important as the number of days that the child would be left alone in a small teepee that was located in a specific area.

Under her dad's watchful eye, Lilly had fasted and stayed awake for one entire day before arriving at the Sioux camp.

Lilly knew that while in training, Navy SEALS stayed awake for five days and nights in a row. Constantly moving and using caffeine wadded in food and stuffed inside the cheek were some ways they were able to stay awake. But the true secret for their success was their navy buddies.

Navy buddies motivated each other to stay the course because only four hours of spaced sleep were permitted.

But Lilly would be alone at the camp, and she was already sleepy. At the reservation's camp area, Lilly had been advised to ignore her first dream and continue dreaming. So alone in the small teepee, for an undisclosed amount of time, Lilly continued to fast and try to stay awake. Soon exhausted, Lilly fell asleep and dreamt. After the first dream that Lilly ignored, a second dream happened.

Awakening, Lilly didn't like the second dream, so she relaxed and fell asleep and dreamt. Once again, the second dream persisted. She was now in the dream world of her subconscious mind where her brain needed to be picked.

Animal power in a person's dream is equal to an individual associating with that animal, bird, or marine life. And Lilly loved all birds.

Sport teams' names associate the team in the same manner. Cubs, Falcons, Hawks, Eagles, Gators, Bulls, Rams, Bucks, Longhorns, Sharks, and Broncos are some identities sport teams chose. Then, Lilly had a fourth dream.

Lilly desired to marry one day. Beauty was usually the first attraction for males. The desire to marry and have a family often trumped her obsession with her loss and her grief and her purpose in life. So naturally, she had to first deal with her fear of muscles.

When Lilly awoke, the medicine woman was by her side with a bowl of soup. As Lilly slowly sipped the broth, the medicine woman asked her to describe her last dream.

What did Lilly fear? Lilly was deeply afraid of developing muscles.

In her last dream, Lilly saw herself looking into a clear pond of water. That was when she noticed the medicine woman throwing stones into the pond. Soon, Lilly's image became distorted, so she stood up and began throwing stones into the water to erase the image that had muscles enlarging in the moving waves.

But Lilly's stones only skipped over the surface of the water, while the frequencies from her shouts caused waves to rub against her reflection, doubling her muscles and their size.

Lilly was now in the moment—reality. She had been thinking in extremes. She was confident but feared being judged, especially since she was taller than her friends. Suddenly, Lilly recalled hugging the tall medicine woman when they had first met. Her blood sister was attractive, tall, and muscular. At last, muscles were beautiful and basically part of the human anatomy.

"Muscles are extremely important, Lilly. Around 30 to 40 percent of a healthy body is made up of skeletal muscles. By the way, Lilly, the more muscle mass you have, the stronger your bones will be."

While mounting their horses, the medicine woman suggested returning to the reservation to discuss the fear behind Lilly's loss, saying, "You seem to think selecting science as a career is disloyal to your father's love for the arts. I believe your father would have wanted you to have psychological health and not be frozen in memories."

While touching Lilly's hand, she added, "Mental health is important in every stage of life. In order for you to help others and our Earth, you will need to be psychologically healthy. I can help you with that and your life's purpose—your gift to the world."

Approaching the reservation, Lilly saw her horse's shadow moving in the opposite direction.

*Special appreciation and thanks go to:*

1. Google
2. Active and retired military and their families
3. Native Americans
4. Dreams
5. Muscles

*Warning:*

Do not attempt to stay awake as Lilly had done. She was under her dad's supervision and later monitored by his Sioux's medicine woman. Remember, this is only a story.

Printed in the United States
By Bookmasters